Dan and the Hong Kong Mystery

Richard MacAndrew

About this Book

For the Student

 Listen to the story and do some activities on your Audio CD
Talk about the story
beat• When you see the blue dot you can check the word in the glossary
K Prepare for Cambridge English: Key (KET) for Schools

For the Teacher

 A state-of-the-art interactive learning environment with 1000s of free online self-correcting activities for your chosen readers.

Go to our Readers Resource site for information on using readers and downloadable Resource Sheets, photocopiable Worksheets and Answer Keys. Plus free sample tracks from the story.

www.helblingreaders.com
For lots of great ideas on using Graded Readers consult Reading Matters, the Teacher's Guide to using Helbling Readers.

Level 3 Structures

Present continuous for future	Cardinal / ordinal numbers
Present perfect	One / ones
Present perfect versus past simple	Reflexive pronouns
Should / shouldn't (advice and obligation)	Indefinite pronouns
Must / should	*Too* plus adjective
Need to / have to	*Not* plus adjective plus *enough*
Will	Relative pronouns *who, which* and *that*
Ever / never	Prepositions of time, place and movement
Would like	
So do I / neither do I	
Question tags	

Structures from lower levels are also included

Contents

	Before Reading	6
1	Breakfast with Sue's grandparents	15
2	A walk around Hong Kong	19
3	Learning more about ivory	26
4	Who is talking to Laura Chan and why?	33
5	Finding out who the man is	37
6	Detective work	42
7	Following Makenga and Kimoti	46
8	Who will get away?	54
9	Getting the evidence	60
	After Reading	65

HELBLING DIGITAL

HELBLING e-zone is an inspiring new state-of-the-art, easy-to-use interactive learning environment.

The online self-correcting activities include:
- reading comprehension;
- listening comprehension;
- vocabulary;
- grammar;
- exam preparation.

- **TEACHERS** register free of charge to set up classes and assign individual and class homework sets. Results are provided automatically once the deadline has been reached and detailed reports on performance are available at a click.

- **STUDENTS** test their language skills in a stimulating interactive environment. All activities can be attempted as many times as necessary and full results and feedback are given as soon as the deadline has been reached. Single student access is also available.

FREE INTERACTIVE ONLINE TEACHING AND LEARNING MATERIALS

1000s of free online interactive activities now available for **HELBLING READERS** and your other favourite Helbling Languages publications.

www.helbling-ezone.com
ONLINE ACTIVITIES

blog.helblingreaders.com

NEW

Love reading and readers and can't wait to get your class interested? Have a class library and reading programme but not sure how to take it a step further? The Helbling Readers BLOG is the place for you.

The **Helbling Readers BLOG** will provide you with ideas on setting up and running a Book Club and tips on reading lessons **every week**.

- Book Club
- Worksheets
- Lesson Plans

Subscribe to our **BLOG** and you will never miss out on our updates.

This is Hong Kong.
Dan and Sue are staying at Victoria Peak, on Hong Kong Island. How do they get to Chungking Mansions?

Before Reading

1 Look at these people. You can see Dan, Sue, Laura Chan, Makenga and Michael Li. Listen to the people speaking and then write the correct name by each picture.

2 Work in pairs. Which person do you like best? Why? Which person do you like least? Why?

3 Complete the picture below with words from the box.

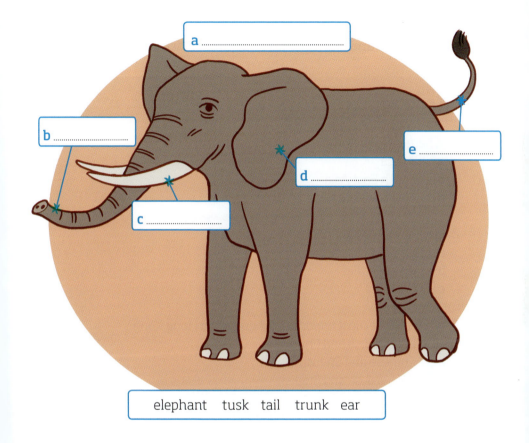

elephant   tusk   tail   trunk   ear

4 What do you know about ivory? Cross out the extra word or words below to make true sentences.
  a Ivory comes from an elephant's trunk/tusks.
  b In many countries people are allowed/not allowed to kill elephants for their tusks.
  c In many countries people are still allowed/not allowed to buy and sell ivory.

5 Work in pairs. What do you think? Is it OK to kill elephants for their tusks? Why?/Why not?

11

Before Reading

1 **Work in pairs and answer these questions. Tick (✔) the correct answer.**

How much do you know about Hong Kong?

1 Where is Hong Kong?
- **a** ☐ Africa
- **b** ☐ South East Asia
- **c** ☐ South America

2 Which country does Hong Kong belong to?
- **a** ☐ China
- **b** ☐ Great Britain
- **c** ☐ Portugal

3 What are the most important languages in Hong Kong?
- **a** ☐ Portuguese and Chinese
- **b** ☐ Chinese and English
- **c** ☐ Portuguese and English

4 How many people live in Hong Kong?
- **a** ☐ about 2 million
- **b** ☐ just under 5 million
- **c** ☐ more than 7 million

5 How many islands are part of Hong Kong?
- **a** ☐ 3
- **b** ☐ about 70
- **c** ☐ more than 200

6 Which is the Hong Kong flag?

a ☐ **b** ☐ **c** ☐

2 Match the verbs from the story with their definitions.

a ☐ reach out
b ☐ slap
c ☐ question
d ☐ wave
e ☐ shake
f ☐ crash open

1 open with a loud noise
2 move quickly from side to side
3 put out a hand
4 hit with your open hand
5 move your hand to show someone something
6 ask about something

3 Use the verbs to complete the sentences.

> crashed open   slapped   reached out
> were questioning   waved   shaking

a 'Really,' said Sue, ... her head angrily, and not sounding interested at all.
b Makenga .... and put his hand round Dan's neck.
c He let go of Dan's neck and .... him hard on the side of the face.
d 'What is he going to say when I tell him about all this.' She .... a hand around the room.
e Yesterday the police .... well-known businessman Joseph Makenga.
f Suddenly the door to the room .... and two police officers stood there.

4 Work in pairs. Look at the pictures below. What do you think is happening in each picture? What is the same in the two pictures? What is different?

13

1 Breakfast with Sue's grandparents

🎧 'Would you like some dim sum•, Dan?' asked Tanya Li, Sue Barrington's grandmother. 'They're a special kind of Chinese food that we have for breakfast sometimes. These ones are chicken. Those ones are fish. And those ones are vegetable. Take one of each, if you like.'

'Thank you,' said Dan, and took one of each. 'They look delicious.'

Dan Parks and Sue Barrington are both 16 years old. They live in the village of Steeple Compton in the south of England. But they are in Hong Kong, visiting Sue's Chinese grandparents. Sue's mother is Chinese and her father is English. Sue's real name is Su Fei, but everybody calls her Sue.

'Sue?' asked Tanya Li, offering her the plate.

'Oh, yes please,' said Sue. 'I love dim sum. Mum sometimes makes them on Sundays.'

Her grandmother smiled. She was short, with black hair and round glasses.

Just then Michael Li, Sue's grandfather, came into the kitchen. He was short too, with a friendly face. He was also wearing glasses, and was dressed for work in a light-coloured suit and a white shirt.

'Hello, you two,' he said. 'Did you sleep well?'

'Yes, thank you,' said Dan and Sue together.

Michael turned on the radio.

'… and yesterday there was some important news about ivory•. This is Andrew Wong from the Department of Conservation•, "We in Hong Kong feel strongly about the buying and selling of ivory.

GLOSSARY

- **Department of Conservation:** environmental part of government
- **dim sum:** Chinese dish
- **ivory:** hard white material from elephants' tusks

15

"We feel we should do everything possible to stop the unnecessary and illegal• killing of elephants. Around 25,000 elephants die every year for the ivory in their tusks•. This cannot continue. The government• has decided to destroy 29 tonnes of ivory this year..."'

'How much is 29 tonnes, Granddad?' asked Sue.

Michael turned the radio down.

'It's a lot,' he replied. '29,000 kilograms.'

'And why does the government have so much ivory?' asked Dan.

'Well, you are not allowed to bring ivory into Hong Kong any more,' explained Michael. 'It's illegal. But some people try and bring it in because you can make a lot of money selling it. When they catch someone trying to bring ivory into Hong Kong, they take the ivory away and the government keeps it.'

'But it's terrible to kill elephants,' said Sue, 'so why do so many people want ivory?'

Michael smiled.

'I'll show you,' he said. He turned the radio off and left the room. A couple of minutes later he came back with something in his hand. He put it on the table in front of Sue and Dan.

GLOSSARY

- **government:** group of people who control a country
- **illegal:** against the law
- **tusk:**

'Ivory hasn't always been illegal,' he explained. 'In fact, even today there are some shops where you can buy ivory legally•.'

He pointed to the thing on the table.

'That is legal ivory,' he said, smiling. 'Actually my great-grandfather made that.'

'Wow!' said Dan.

'It's beautiful,' said Sue.

'That's the point,' said Michael. 'It is beautiful. People can make beautiful things out of ivory. And Chinese people have always loved things like that. We believe ivory brings good luck. But a lot of people don't know where it comes from. They don't know how many elephants die every year.'

'They said on the radio 25,000 a year. That's terrible,' said Sue.

Ivory
What do you think is the difference between legal and illegal ivory?

• **legally:** allowed by the law

'Yes,' agreed Tanya, putting some more dim sum on the table. 'But the government is finally doing something. Mainly because everyone in Hong Kong wants them to do something. Even the schoolchildren.'

'What do you mean?' asked Sue.

'Well,' began Tanya, 'schoolchildren all over Hong Kong have written letters to the government. In fact, in the school where I teach, 500 children got together and sent a letter from all of them to the government. They asked the government to stop all ivory trading•.'

'That's great,' said Sue.

'Wonderful,' said Dan.

'Yes,' agreed Tanya, smiling. 'And the teachers didn't ask the children to do this. The children did it all by themselves.'

'That's so cool,' said Dan.

He looked at Sue.

'We must find out more about ivory while we're here in Hong Kong. Then maybe, when we get back to England, we can do something too.'

'That's a good idea,' agreed Sue. But she knew Dan. It sounded simple, but it probably wasn't.

GLOSSARY

• **trading:** buying and selling

2 A walk around Hong Kong

Sue's grandparents lived in an apartment in a building on the Peak. Victoria Peak, usually simply called the Peak, is a large hill on Hong Kong Island where there are some very beautiful old houses and many new apartment blocks. Michael Li worked for a large Hong Kong bank, and Tanya Li taught English in a secondary school.

'We're both going to work soon,' said Tanya, 'but I should be back by three o'clock. Until then you've got the day to yourselves.'

She looked across at Dan.

'Sue comes here every year so she knows her way around,' she told him. 'She can take you sightseeing this morning, if you like.'

'Yes, please,' said Dan, looking at Sue. 'I've never been anywhere like this before and we're only here for a short time. I want to see as much as possible.'

'Come on then,' said Sue. 'First of all, we'll go up to the top of the Peak. You can look out over almost all of Hong Kong from there and you'll see what a wonderful place it is.'

Fifteen minutes later Dan and Sue were standing on the Peak Tower looking over Hong Kong Island and across Victoria Harbour to Kowloon. The weather was very warm and they were both wearing light clothes. Sue pointed to some of the famous sights• of Hong Kong: the Star Ferry• that travels between Hong Kong Island and Kowloon; Causeway Bay; the Peninsula Hotel on Kowloon, and on both sides of the harbour, hundreds of tall office blocks, apartment blocks and hotels.

Next they took the Peak Tram• down to a part of the city called Central, and they started to walk through the streets.

'Where are we going?' asked Dan.

'Nowhere,' said Sue, laughing. 'Let's walk for a bit. Hong Kong is so different from England. Sometimes I like to walk around and enjoy the noise and the colours and the people.'

'That sounds a great idea,' said Dan, a big smile on his face.

GLOSSARY

- **ferry:** boat that takes people from one place to another
- **sights:** interesting or beautiful parts of a town or city
- **tram:** vehicle like a bus that runs on rails

They walked and walked. After half an hour they stopped for a coffee and some cake.

'This is such an amazing place,' said Dan, as he ate a Chinese rice cake. 'Thank you so much for inviting me to come with you. It's so different from England and from Europe.'

Sue smiled at him.

'I mean, there are so many people,' continued Dan. 'And I love the Chinese writing everywhere. I can't understand it but I still love it.'

Sue laughed.

'I don't understand it either,' she said. 'I can speak some Chinese but I can't read it.'

'And I love the bright colours,' said Dan, 'and the shops selling all sorts of different things. And some of the things… well, I don't know what they are!'

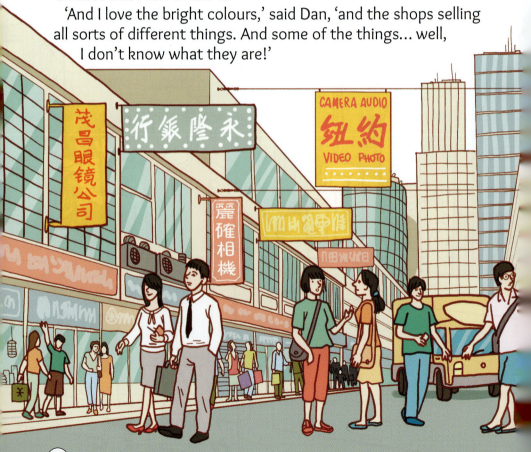

Sue laughed again.

They finished their tea and cakes and started walking again. They went through a part of the city called Wanchai, full of bars and restaurants, on to Causeway Bay, and then into a street called Jardine's Bazaar. There were all kinds of shops. They stopped outside a food shop.

'What are those?' asked Dan, pointing at some strange brown egg-like things.

'They're called "100-year eggs",' said Sue. 'They are old, they're not really 100 years old. Probably only a few months. You eat them. Some people really like them, but I think they're horrible.'

Just then Dan noticed the shop next door.

'Look!' he said. 'It's an ivory shop. Wow! Look here! There are animals and boxes and people and all sorts of things made of ivory.'

Dan and Sue looked at all the things in the window. They could see a woman inside the shop.

'Let's go inside,' said Dan.

'Why?' asked Sue. 'You don't want to buy anything, do you?'

'Of course not,' replied Dan. 'But I'm interested. And I'd like to talk to that woman.'

Sue gave Dan a strange look• as he opened the door. She knew Dan well. He sometimes thought he was a detective. He was actually quite good at being a detective.

'Well, he certainly thinks he's a detective right now,' thought Sue, shaking• her head. 'Why does he want to talk to her?'

Then she followed him into the shop.

Detective

Write a definition of the word 'detective'.
Use a dictionary if necessary.

GLOSSARY

- **look:** how your face shows your feelings

- **shaking:** moving quickly from side to side

3 Learning more about ivory

'Yes, yes, this shop is a legal ivory shop,' Sue heard the woman say in reply to Dan's opening question. 'We are licensed•.'

Sue saw a box of business cards on a table. They read 'Laura Chan — licensed ivory trader•'.

'But how do I know you are licensed?' asked Dan.

Laura Chan pointed behind her. Dan and Sue looked at Laura Chan's licence• on the wall.

LICENCE

Laura Chan

is licensed
by
The Government of Hong Kong
to sell legal ivory

Simon Ho
Department of Conservation

GLOSSARY

- **licence:** piece of paper giving official permission
- **licensed:** with official permission to do something
- **trader:** someone who buys and sells things

'I have that piece of paper from the government,' said Laura Chan, still pointing. 'And then, when someone buys a piece of ivory, I give them a certificate•. The certificate has a photograph of the piece. The photo shows you what it looks like: an elephant, or a bird, or a person, for example. And the certificate tells you that the ivory is legal.'

Laura Chan turned and took an ivory dragon• and a piece of paper from the shelf behind her.

'Look,' she said, showing Dan and Sue the dragon, the certificate, and the photo of the dragon on the certificate.

'When you buy a piece of ivory,' she continued, 'you must always check the certificate very carefully. Sometimes people try and use old certificates with new pieces of illegal ivory. You must check that the certificate has the right photo.'

Certificate

Do you have any certificates?
What are they for?

🗩 Tell a friend.

• **certificate:** piece of paper that shows something is true

• **dragon:** animal in stories with wings and a tail, and with fire coming out of its mouth

'But what exactly is legal ivory?' asked Dan. 'I mean, isn't all ivory illegal now?'

'Well,' began Laura Chan, 'ivory only became illegal in 1989 so anything older than that is OK. And it is still possible to buy ivory legally in South Africa – but that too is old ivory from before 1989.'

'I see,' said Dan, thinking for a moment. Then he asked: 'But you can buy ivory legally – so why do people buy illegal ivory?'

Laura Chan smiled.

'Chinese people love ivory,' she replied. 'They buy ivory because it brings good luck. And they buy ivory because it is expensive. It shows that you have a lot of money. Legal ivory is really expensive. Illegal ivory is cheaper.'

Then she laughed.

'But, of course, ivory is ivory. It all looks the same. So nobody knows what it cost,' she said.

Legal or illegal?
Is this explanation the same as yours?
Go back to page 17 to check.

Dan and Sue thanked Laura Chan for her help and left the shop. Outside Sue turned to Dan.

'What was all that about?' she asked. 'Why were you asking so many questions about ivory?'

'I'm interested,' replied Dan. 'I told you. I think we should try and help in some way when we get home.'

'Yes, but…' began Sue, but Dan suddenly took her by the arm.

'Look,' he said. Sue turned to see what Dan was looking at. A tall African man was opening the door to the ivory shop. He was wearing a suit and carrying a bag in his hand.

'What's an African man doing here?' he asked.

'He's probably a tourist,' said Sue.

'Sue,' said Dan, surprise in his voice. 'Where do elephants come from?'

'Well, Africa,' began Sue, 'but…'

'Come on,' said Dan, walking towards the shop window. 'I want to see what's happening.'

4 Who is talking to Laura Chan and why?

Sue followed Dan to the shop window. This time they weren't looking at the pieces of ivory in the window. They were watching Laura Chan and the African man talking. Laura Chan and the man spoke together for a few minutes.

'I'm going to go in and tell her I forgot to ask something,' said Dan. 'I want to hear their conversation.'

Sue took Dan's arm and held it.

'No, Dan,' she said. 'Don't be stupid. You don't know who he is. Anyway, they'll stop talking when they see you.'

'But…' began Dan.

'No,' said Sue. 'Stay here and make sure they don't see us.'

'All right,' said Dan, but he wasn't happy.

Laura Chan was smiling at the man and continuing to talk. Then the man put his bag on the table and opened it. He took something out and showed it to Laura Chan. She looked at it, turning it over in her hands. She gave it back to the man. He put it back in his bag.

'What was that?' asked Dan.

'I don't know,' answered Sue. 'I couldn't really see it. It looked white. So maybe a piece of ivory. I mean, it is an ivory shop.'

The man seemed to be agreeing with Laura Chan. She smiled again. Then they shook hands.

'Quick,' said Sue. 'He's going to leave. Let's go to the other side of the street.'

Dan and Sue moved quickly across the street and began to take a lot of interest in some clothes in another shop window.

They heard the door of the ivory shop open and close. Dan turned round with his phone in his hand. The African was standing in the shop doorway. He looked both ways up and down the street.

Sue could see what Dan was doing.

'Dan, no!' she said angrily. 'Don't take a photo! He'll see you.'

'It's OK,' said Dan quietly. Without moving his phone, he quickly took a few photos. He moved the phone around a little between each photo to make sure he got a picture of the man.

'He doesn't know I'm taking photos,' said Dan, looking at Sue and not at the man. 'And I should get at least one good one of him.'

'Dan! Stop it!' said Sue again. She took him by the arm and turned him round to look in the shop window.

'Look at that dress,' she said in her normal voice. 'I really like it. What do you think of it?'

'Nice,' said Dan, not really looking. Out of the corner of his eye, he was watching the man walk down Jardine's Bazaar towards Hennessy Road.

Dan looked at his phone, then showed it to Sue.

'Look,' he said. 'I've got a really good picture of him.'

Photo

When is it right or wrong to take a photo of someone?

Discuss in small groups.

'Really?' said Sue, shaking her head angrily, and not sounding interested at all. 'And what are you going to do with the picture?'

'I'm not really sure,' replied Dan. 'But there are some websites that find photos or pictures for you. You put a photo in and the website finds that photo, or ones like it, and tells you where you can find them on the Internet.'

Dan put his phone back in his pocket.

'And I'm going to have a look at websites about elephants and about buying and selling ivory,' he continued.

'Well,' said Sue. 'I don't want any adventures while we're here. Not like our holiday on the island of Bute. This is Hong Kong. Not the UK.'

Then she looked at her watch.

'Come on,' she said. 'We should start going back. My grandmother will be home soon.'

Slowly they started walking back towards Central and the Peak Tram. Dan was still drinking in• the sights and sounds• of the East, and thinking about the man from Africa. Sue was also deep in thought•.

'Why does Dan have to ask so many questions? How can I stop him from having one of his crazy adventures? Why did I ask him to come with me?'

Well, she knew the answer to the last question. He was kind, and they had a lot fun together. But he really made her cross• sometimes.

GLOSSARY

- **cross:** angry; annoyed
- **deep in thought:** thinking hard
- **drinking in:** enjoying
- **sounds:** noises

5 Finding out who the man is

Back at the Li's apartment on the Peak, Tanya Li was not home yet. Dan took out his tablet, sat on the sofa in the living room and started searching• the Internet. Sue got them both some lemonade from the fridge and sat next to him, watching. Dan found a lot of a websites with general information about the illegal killing of elephants and about the buying and selling of illegal ivory. He and Sue looked at the *Born Free* website and the *Bloody Ivory* website. They learned more about how many elephants die every year, how people kill them and how they take their ivory tusks.

'This is terrible,' said Sue, as she read more and more. 'How can people do these things to such lovely animals?'

'It's horrible,' agreed Dan. 'We really have to do something when we get home.'

Sue smiled at him.

'Yes,' she said. 'I think so too. Maybe we can start our own website and get money to send to Africa.'

Then Dan found the *Ban• Ivory Trading* website. A lot of the information was the same as on the other websites. But there was also a 'library' of newspaper articles•. Dan started to look through the articles. Suddenly his eyes opened wide.

'Look at this,' he said to Sue, pointing at the article and the photo. 'It's him. It's the man from the ivory shop.'

'So it is,' said Sue.

GLOSSARY

- **articles:** pieces of writing in a newspaper or magazine
- **ban:** stop something happening
- **searching:** looking on

They read the article together.

Makenga questioned by police

Following the discovery of two tonnes of ivory in a building on the edge• of the city, Johannesburg police were yesterday questioning• well-known businessman Joseph Makenga. Makenga owns• a number of companies throughout• southern Africa. Yesterday he spent ten hours at Johannesburg police station. Police questioned him about how the ivory came to be in a building owned by one of his companies and what he himself knew about it. As Makenga left the police station yesterday evening, he said: 'I have done nothing wrong. I have told the police everything I know. I have no idea who put the ivory in that building. Yes, I am a businessman, but I have nothing to do with the ivory trade.'

'Well, he's clearly not telling the truth here,' said Dan pointing at the article. 'He says he has nothing to do with the ivory trade but we saw him in an ivory shop this morning. I'm going to email the website.'

Sue said nothing.

Dan started typing an email on his tablet. He explained about Makenga and the ivory shop. He looked at the website, found the email address for BIT• and sent his message.

GLOSSARY

- **BIT:** organisation Ban Ivory Trading
- **edge:** outer part of something
- **owns:** has
- **questioning:** asking questions to
- **throughout:** in every part of

Two minutes later there was a reply.

From:	Kyle Pienaar kyle@bit.com
To:	Dan Parks d.parks71199@rocketmail.com
Re:	Joseph Makenga

Hi Dan

Thank you for your email and the photo. The information you sent is extremely useful to our organisation. We are very interested in Joseph Makenga. The South African police have questioned him three times in the last year but they have not found any evidence against him. Either he is giving money to some police officers, or he is very careful. We also know about Laura Chan. The Hong Kong police are very interested in her. She is a licensed ivory trader but the police believe she trades in illegal ivory too. But, like Makenga, there is no evidence against her. I will make sure that the right people see your photo. As you say, it shows that he was not telling the truth outside the police station.

Makenga often works with a man called Peter Kamoti. I'm sending you a photo of him. We would really like to know where these men are staying in Hong Kong but… do NOT talk to them and do NOT go near them. They are very dangerous.

Thank you for your help.

Kyle Pienaar

GLOSSARY

- **evidence:** anything that shows something is true
- **extremely:** very

'Wow!' said Dan, and he showed the email to Sue.

Sue read it.

'We have to tell my grandparents about this,' said Sue. 'Or show it to the police.'

'Well, your grandparents can't do anything about it,' said Dan. 'And I'm sure BIT will tell the police. Kyle says they're going to send my photo to the "right people". He must mean the police.'

'Well, I think we should tell the police too,' said Sue.

'But they think Makenga is paying some police officers,' replied Dan. 'We don't want to tell the wrong ones. Then Makenga will get away•.'

'Hmm,' said Sue, thinking. 'Maybe you're right. But we're not going to go anywhere near these people. We'll stay away• from them, won't we?'

'OK,' said Dan. But that's not what he was thinking.

Away

What do you think Dan will do?

Will Dan stay away or stop Makenga from getting away?

• **get away:** escape

• **stay away:** not go near

6 Detective work

🎧 The next day Michael and Tanya Li both left for work again soon after breakfast.

'Come on,' said Dan to Sue. 'Let's go out. I want to go back to Laura Chan's ivory shop and wait for Makenga.'

'Dan!' said Sue. 'We can't do that. The email said these men are dangerous and we shouldn't go near them.'

'We don't have to go near them,' replied Dan. 'We can keep a long way away• and watch them. It shouldn't be difficult to find out where they are staying. And that'll be really helpful for BIT.'

Sue looked at Dan.

'We can't,' she said. 'We mustn't. It's really not a good idea.'

Dan put a hand on her shoulder.

'I think we should go,' said Dan. 'And anyway, I'm going to.'

'OK,' said Sue. 'Well, then I'll come too. Just to make sure you don't do anything stupid.'

Half an hour later Dan and Sue were sitting in a small café on Jardine's Bazaar watching the entrance to Laura Chan's ivory shop.

A few people went into the shop and came out but not Makenga. Dan and Sue sat, and read, and drank tea, and waited. Time passed. At about 12 o'clock Dan looked up.

'There,' he said.

Sue looked up too.

'Makenga,' said Dan. 'And Kamoti.'

Dan's phone was on the table. He quickly took some photos as the two men went into the shop. Makenga had a large red and green bag in his hand. Kamoti closed the shop door behind them.

GLOSSARY

- **a long way away:** far; a long distance away

Dan and Sue waited.

A few minutes later the men came out without the bag. They were smiling and laughing. They started walking towards Hennessy Road. Quickly Dan took another photo.

'Come on,' said Dan. 'Let's follow them.'

'Dan!' said Sue. 'We...'

'It'll be fine,' said Dan. 'Don't worry.'

'We have to keep away from them,' said Sue.

'We will,' said Dan. 'We'll let them get a long way ahead•. They won't see us. They won't even know we are following them.'

Sue gave Dan a hard• look but he left the café and started following the two men. Sue went out quickly after him. The men were laughing and joking as they walked along Hennessy Road. They stopped and looked in shop windows from time to time•. Dan and Sue stopped too. Dan took his phone out and emailed BIT.

From:	Dan Parks d.parks71199@rocketmail.com
To:	Kyle Pienaar kyle@bit.com
Re:	Joseph Makenga

I'm sending you photos of Makenga and Kamoti going in and coming out of Laura Chan's ivory shop this morning. We are following them and will let you know the name of their hotel.

Dan Parks

GLOSSARY

- **ahead:** in front
- **from time to time:** sometimes; not regularly
- **hard:** (here) long and serious

The two men continued walking into Central and to the Star Ferry.

'They're going over to Kowloon on the ferry,' said Sue. 'We need to stop following them. They'll see us on the ferry.'

'It'll be fine,' said Dan. 'Don't worry. We'll sit in a different part of the boat.'

The men got on the ferry. Dan and Sue followed.

The men went upstairs.

Dan and Sue stayed downstairs.

Dan's phone made a sound as an email came in. He read it.

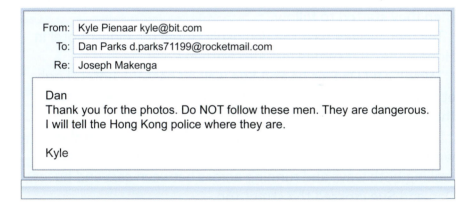

'What's that?' asked Sue.

'An email from BIT,' answered Dan. 'They're saying they got my photos.'

He put his phone back in his pocket and smiled at Sue.

'She doesn't need to see that,' he thought. 'These men will never see us.'

45

7 Following Makenga and Kimoti

The ferry arrived at Kowloon. Dan and Sue got off before the two men.

'Let's look like we're tourists,' said Dan to Sue. He took out his phone and took some photos while they waited for the men to get off.

After a couple of minutes they saw Makenga and Kamoti coming off the ferry. The men were still laughing and joking as they started walking along Salisbury Road.

Dan and Sue let them get about a hundred metres ahead and then they started to follow.

The men walked past the Peninsula Hotel, the oldest hotel in Hong Kong, and turned left into Nathan Road.

'Wow!' said Dan, as he and Sue walked past the hotel. 'Look at that!' There were ten black Rolls Royce cars parked outside the hotel.

Dan and Sue turned the corner behind the men. Then they watched as the men crossed the road further up the street, looking both ways and running across between cars and buses. Dan and Sue crossed the street too.

Dan took out his phone again and sent another email.

Follow

Go back to pages 8 and 9. Follow Dan and Sue's adventure on the map.

From:	Dan Parks d.parks71199@rocketmail.com
To:	Kyle Pienaar kyle@bit.com
Re:	Joseph Makenga

Makenga and Kamoti are walking up Nathan Road.

Dan

The men walked towards a tall tower block on the right-hand side of the road. Sue was looking at the map on her phone.

'That building is Chungking Mansions,' she said.

'Quick,' said Dan. 'We need to know which floor they are going to.'

'No, Dan!' said Sue. 'We'll be too close.'

But Dan took Sue's hand and started running, half-pulling her, towards the entrance.

As they arrived at the entrance, they saw Makenga and Kamoti standing in the lift, still talking to each other. Neither of the men looked in Dan and Sue's direction as the lift doors started to close.

Dan looked at the lights above the lift. There were 17 floors. The light stopped at the 15th.

'That's where they are,' he said. 'The 15th floor.'

He pushed the button to call the lift. As it started to come down he sent another email.

'What are you doing?' asked Sue, surprised. 'We're not going up in the lift.'

'Just to have a quick look,' said Dan. 'They'll be in an apartment or an office. They won't see us. Then we'll come back down. I promise.'

The lift doors opened. Sue took Dan's arm and tried to stop him getting in the lift. He pushed her hand away and got in.

Stop

Why does Sue try and stop Dan?
What is the best thing to do?
Go up in the lift or stop?

'You stay here,' he said. 'I'll go.'
But Sue got in the lift, with a dark• look on her face.
Dan pushed the button for the 15th floor.
'I don't like this,' said Sue.
'It'll be fine,' said Dan. 'They have no idea who we are.'
The lift went up.
It stopped.
As the doors began to open, Dan's phone made a sound. Another email. He left the phone in his pocket.

Look

Practise giving these different looks with a friend.

- ☐ worried look
- ☐ strange look
- ☐ hard look
- ☐ dark look
- ☐ happy look

GLOSSARY

• **dark:** angry and worried

The doors opened wide. The two men were standing there, waiting. Kamoti took Dan by the arm, Makenga took Sue. They pulled them out of the lift.

'Hey!' shouted Dan and tried to fight back, but Kamoti was much too strong.

The men pulled the two teenagers into a small room near the lift. It looked like some kind of office. Makenga found some rope•. He threw some to Kamoti and they tied Dan and Sue to chairs. Kamoti then found their phones and took them away. He looked at Sue's, then at Dan's. Then he laughed.

'Ha!' he said. 'You've just had an email. It says: "Keep away from those men. I repeat – do not go near them."' He continued to look at their phones, doing something with them.

Makenga smiled at Dan. It was not a nice smile.

'That was good advice, young man. But it's too late now,' he said.

GLOSSARY

• **rope:** strong type of material used to tie things

8 Who will get away?

Dan pulled at the ropes around his body. He looked across at Sue. He could see she was trying hard not to cry. But she was angry too. She looked across at him.

'I told you, you stupid boy,' her eyes seemed to say. 'I said we should stay downstairs.'

For once Dan thought Sue was right.

Dan pulled again at his ropes.

'Untie• me. And her. Let us go,' he said. 'You can't keep us here.'

Makenga laughed. Then the smile disappeared from his face. 'Why were you following us?' he asked.

'We weren't,' said Dan.

Makenga reached out• and put his hand round Dan's neck.

'Don't play games with me,' he said angrily. He looked at Kamoti.

'Ring Laura Chan,' he said. 'We need to talk to her.'

Kamoti took a phone from his pocket and started to make a call. Makenga looked back at Dan.

'You were following us,' he said. 'I saw you yesterday outside Laura Chan's shop. And again today. You followed us to the Star Ferry and then came across on the same boat as us.'

GLOSSARY

- **reached out**: put out a hand
- **untie**: undo the rope

Dan thought fast.

'We weren't following you,' he said. 'We went to Laura Chan's shop to have another look at some ivory. That's why we were there yesterday – looking at ivory. Then we came here to visit her aunt.' He looked at Sue as he said this. 'She lives here in Chungking Mansions. We pushed the wrong button on the lift. She's on the 14th floor.'

'I don't believe you,' said Makenga.

He looked at Kamoti.

'Well?' he asked.

'She's not answering,' replied Kamoti.

A worried look appeared on Makenga's face but then quickly disappeared.

He let go of Dan's neck and slapped• him hard on the side of the face.

'Ouch!' Dan cried out, trying hard not to cry. The slap hurt a lot.

'The next time I'll hit the girl,' said Makenga. 'Now answer the question. Why were you following us?'

Dan looked at Sue. Her face was white as snow. She looked frightened, very frightened. He mustn't let Makenga hit her.

'What will I say to her grandparents?' he thought. 'What will I say to her parents?'

He opened his mouth to tell Makenga the truth. It was the only thing to do.

'Well, we saw you at Laura Chan's shop,' he began, 'and...'

There were loud noises outside the room: people running, doors opening and closing, shouting.

Makenga and Kamoti looked at each other.

Suddenly the door to the room crashed open• and two police officers – a man and a women – stood there pointing guns at Makenga and Kamoti.

'Sergeant Wong, Hong Kong police,' said the woman. 'Put your hands on your heads, very very slowly.'

Makenga and Kamoti moved slowly, putting their hands on top of their heads.

GLOSSARY

• **crashed open:** opened with a loud noise

• **slapped:** hit with an open hand

'I'm very glad you are here,' said Makenga, looking at Wong and thinking quickly. 'I want to report• these children. They followed us here from Causeway Bay. They were behind us all the way to the Star Ferry.

'They came across on the ferry with us and then they followed us here. They even came up in the lift to this floor. I'm very angry about this and I'd like you to take them away, please.'

'It's true,' said Dan, turning in his chair to look at the police officers. 'We were following them. They are illegal ivory traders.'

'Yes,' added Sue, already beginning to look happier now that the police officers were in the room. 'We saw them at Laura Chan's ivory shop in Jardine's Bazaar.'

Makenga laughed and shook his head a little.

'Kids!' he said. 'Where do they get their ideas from?'

Think

Can you think quickly like Dan on page 55 and Makenga on this page?
Think of a time when you had to think quickly.

Tell a friend about it.

— GLOSSARY

• **report:** tell the police about a crime

Wong smiled.

'You will find out,' she said. 'We know about these two "kids". The organisation *Ban Ivory Trading* has told us everything about them. We know you were at Laura Chan's. We have just caught her. She was leaving her shop with a large red and green bag full of ivory.'

Makenga laughed again.

'That is nothing to do with me or my friend here,' he said waving• a hand at Kamoti. 'If this Laura Chan has illegal ivory, that is her problem. I have never heard of her. I don't even know who she is.'

'That's not true,' said Dan. 'These men were there.'

'We saw them,' said Sue.

Makenga shook his head, smiling.

'This is my office when I come to Hong Kong,' he said. 'You can look all around it. You won't find any ivory here. I'm staying at The Peninsula Hotel. You can search my room there. You won't find any ivory. There is no evidence of ivory. There is no evidence that I know Laura Chan. Take these kids away and leave me and my friend alone.'

Dan and Sue looked at each other as two more police officers came into the room and started untying them.

'Surely Makenga can't get away with this?' thought Dan.

Then suddenly he remembered. His phone.

GLOSSARY

• **waving:** moving your hand to show someone something

9 Getting the evidence

'I've got a photo of them going into the shop with that bag,' he said. 'And another photo of them coming out without the bag.'

'Show me,' said Wong.

Then she spoke to the two police officers.

'Put handcuffs• on the men,' she said.

'He's got our phones,' said Dan, pointing at Kamoti.

One of the police officers put handcuffs on Kamoti and then searched his pockets. She found three phones.

'That's mine,' said Dan, pointing at his.

The policewoman gave it to him. Dan started to look for the photo. After a minute or two, he looked up at Kamoti.

'Hey! Where are my photos?' he said. 'What have you done with them?'

Kamoti and Makenga looked at each other. There was the tiniest smile on Kamoti's lips.

'He's deleted all my photos,' said Dan.

'There never were any photos,' said Kamoti. He looked at Sergeant Wong. 'My friend told you. We were not at this Laura Chan's. We don't know who she is. These kids have made it all up•.'

Dan looked at Wong.

'They were there,' he said. 'I promise you.'

Wong looked a little worried for a moment.

GLOSSARY

- **handcuffs:** see picture
- **made it all up:** invented it

60

'Dan,' said Sue. 'BIT.'
'Of course,' he said. Quickly he wrote an email.

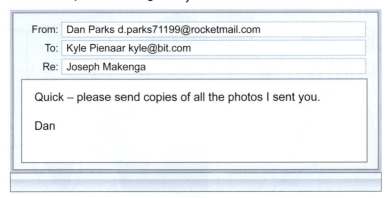

He pressed 'send'. Then he looked at Wong and smiled.
'Two minutes,' he said to her.
'OK,' she replied.
He saw Makenga and Kamoti look at each other again. This time they looked worried.
Dan's phone made a sound – an email arriving. He opened the email. It was the photos from BIT. He moved his finger across the phone looking at the photos. He looked at Makenga and Kamoti and smiled. Then he gave his phone to Wong.
'You'll find everything you need there,' he said.
Wong looked through the photos.
'I'll need to keep your phone,' she said to Dan. 'And yours.' She looked at Sue.
'OK,' said Dan.
'OK,' said Sue.
'Take those men away,' she said to the other officers. The police officers took Kamoti and Makenga out of the room.

Wong looked at Sue and then at Dan.

'And I need to take you two home,' she said. 'Where are you staying?'

'We're staying with my grandparents on the Peak,' said Sue. 'My grandfather is Michael Li.'

'Ah!' said Wong, putting a finger to her lips. 'And what is he going to say when I tell him about you two? And about all this?' She waved a hand around the room.

Sue's eyes opened wide and she put her hand to her mouth.

'Oh please, no!' she said. 'You can't tell my grandfather about this. He'll tell my parents. And there'll be so much trouble.'

'No,' said Dan. 'Please don't tell him. You can take us to the end of the road and we'll walk back to the house. But please don't say anything to him. I mean, we have helped you… a lot.'

Wong looked from Sue to Dan and back again.

'OK,' said Wong. 'We'll do it your way. I know where your grandfather lives, I'll take you to the road and you can walk home.'

'Thank you,' said Sue.

'But you'll have to come to the police station sometime,' she said. 'I need you to tell me everything that has happened.'

'Oh no!' said Dan and Sue together.

She looked at Sue.

'It's all right,' she said. 'I'll call your grandparents and say we found your phones on the Star Ferry and someone gave them in to the police. So you'll need to come down and get them.'

'But,' Wong continued, 'you must promise me one thing.'
'Yes?' said Dan.
'Stay away from ivory shops,' she said. 'And don't follow anyone else. You were very lucky today. Kyle Pienaar works closely with us. He was very worried about you. He knows how dangerous Makenga is. He told you to stay away and you didn't.'
'Yes,' said Dan. 'I'm sorry.'
'Good,' said Wong. 'Promise?'
'Yes,' said Dan.
Wong looked at Sue.
'Yes,' said Sue, giving Dan a very black look.
'Oh no!' thought Dan. 'I'm in trouble now.'
'Good,' said Wong. 'And, by the way – well done! We've wanted Makenga and Laura Chan for a long time. They've been too clever until now.'
She smiled at the teenagers.
'OK,' she said. 'Let's get you back to the Peak.'

After Reading

Personal Response

1 Read each sentence and circle the number that is most true for you.

1 = Not really.   **5** = Definitely.

a I liked the story.
   1   2   3   4   5

b The story was easy to understand.
   1   2   3   4   5

c I think that the story was exciting.
   1   2   3   4   5

d I'd like to read another book about Dan.
   1   2   3   4   5

2 Work in pairs. Discuss these questions.

a Which person in the story do you like the most? Why?
b Which person in the story do you like the least? Why?
c Do you think Dan is clever? Or is he a bit stupid? Why?
d Do you think Dan should listen more to Sue?
e Do you think Sue is too careful? Why?/Why not?

After Reading

Comprehension

1 Are the following sentences true (T) or false (F)? Tick (✔).

		T	F
a	Dan asked Sue to go to Hong Kong with him.	☐	☐
b	Sue always has dim sum for breakfast.	☐	☐
c	About 2,500 elephants die every year because people want their tusks.	☐	☐
d	Michael Li has some illegal ivory.	☐	☐
e	Tanya Li is a teacher.	☐	☐
f	Schoolchildren in Hong Kong are worried about people killing elephants for ivory.	☐	☐
g	Sue takes Dan up to the Peak to see the view over Hong Kong.	☐	☐
h	Sue wants to show Dan Jardine's Bazaar.	☐	☐
i	Sue doesn't like '100-year eggs'.	☐	☐
j	Sue takes Dan into Laura Chan's shop.	☐	☐
k	Dan asks Laura Chan some questions about ivory.	☐	☐
l	Laura Chan is a licensed ivory trader.	☐	☐
m	Dan goes back into Laura Chan's shop to hear the conversation between her and Makenga.	☐	☐
n	Makenga and Laura Chan shake hands.	☐	☐
o	Dan takes a photo of Makenga.	☐	☐

2 Correct the false sentences in Exercise 1.

3 These sentences are about the second half of the story. Put them in the correct order.

a ☐ Dan finds a newspaper article about the man in Laura Chan's shop.

b ☐ Makenga and Kimoti visit Laura Chan's shop.

c ☐1 Dan and Sue go back to Sue's grandparent's apartment.

d ☐ Sergeant Wong takes Dan and Sue back to the Peak.

e ☐ Dan and Sue follow Makenga and Kimoti.

f ☐ Makenga and Kimoti catch Dan and Sue and tie them up.

g ☐ The police take Makenga and Kimoti away.

h ☐ Dan sends his first email to *Ban Ivory Trading*.

i ☐ The police arrive.

j ☐ Dan asks BIT to send him his photos.

k ☐ Kimoti deletes Dan's photos from his phone.

l ☐ Dan and Sue watch the entrance to Laura Chan's shop.

4 Work in pairs. Student A and Student B.

Student A	**Student B**
You are a schoolfriend of Dan (or Sue). They have just come back from Hong Kong. Ask them:	You are Dan (or Sue). You are back home in England. You meet one of your schoolfriends. Tell them about your holiday in Hong Kong. Say:
• if they enjoyed their holiday • what they did • what else happened • how they felt	• what you saw at Laura Chan's • how you followed Makenga and Kimoti • what happened when they caught you • how you felt about it

After Reading

Characters

1 Complete the sentences with the name of a person from the story.

a .... loves dim sum.

b .... works in a bank.

c .... likes to walk around the streets of Hong Kong.

d .... is a licensed ivory trader.

e .... goes into a shop with a bag in his hand.

f .... answers Dan's email to BIT.

g .... takes Dan's phone.

h .... agrees not to talk to Sue's grandparents.

2 Who said what? Match each quote to a person.

☐ Laura Chan ☐ Michael Li ☐ Dan ☐ Sue ☐ Makenga

A That is legal ivory. Actually my great-grandfather made that.

B The certificate tells you that the ivory is legal.

C Dan, no! Don't take a photo! He'll see you.

D These men will never see us.

E You were following us. I saw you yesterday outside Laura Chan's shop.

3 **All about Dan. Answer these questions about Dan.**

a What does Dan think about Hong Kong?

....

b Why does Dan go into Laura Chan's shop?

....

c Why does Dan send his first email to BIT?

....

d Why does Dan want to follow Makenga and Kamoti?

....

e Why doesn't Dan show Sue one of the emails from BIT?

....

f Why does Dan send the final email to BIT?

....

4 **Answer these questions with a name/names.**

a Who wrote to the Hong Kong government asking them to stop ivory trading? ....

b Who is happy to break the law and trade in illegal ivory?

..................., ... and ....

c Who works for an organisation which is trying to stop illegal ivory trading? ....

d Who thinks that following Makenga and Kimoti is dangerous?

.... and ....

e Who sometimes does things without thinking? ....

After Reading

Plot and Theme

1 Complete the newspaper article with appropriate forms of the verbs from the box.

> own catch help be visit be thank tell find question

South China Times

WHO HELPED POLICE TO CATCH ILLEGAL IVORY TRADERS?

Police yesterday **a** .... three illegal ivory traders. Sergeant Jenny Wong of the Hong Kong Police said: 'We are **b** .... three people. Two of them, Mr Joseph Makenga and Mr Peter Kimoti, **c** .... from South Africa. The third person, Ms Laura Chan, **d** .... an ivory shop in Jardine's Bazaar near Causeway Bay.'

When asked how the police **e** .... out about these people, Sergeant Wong said: 'We have **f** .... interested in Ms Chan for some time. And Mr Makenga and Mr Kimoti have **g** .... Hong Kong a number of times recently. We also received help and information from the public, telling us where to find them.'

Unusually the *South China Times* was not able to find out more information about the people who **h** .... the police. 'I'm sorry,' replied Sergeant Wong. 'I cannot give you their names. These people have been extremely helpful but I am not able to **i** .... you any more about them.'

Maybe these people do not want us to know their names, but the *South China Times* would like to **j** .... them for helping to stop the illegal ivory trade.

70

2 The story is about some animals that are in danger. Work in pairs. Complete the questionnaire below.

WHY ARE SOME ANIMALS IN DANGER?

1 Do you know these animals?

```
crocodile
orang-utan
elephant
whale
tiger
panda
rhino
gorilla
```

2 Do you know why some animals are in danger? Write the name of each animal in the correct part of the table.

REASON	ANIMAL(S)
We kill these animals for their skin so we can make bags, shoes, belts, and wallets.	
We kill these animals because they have beautiful skin and we use their bones for medicine.	
We kill these animals for their ivory tusks and because we think that ivory brings good luck.	
We kill these animals for their meat and to make oil from the fat in their bodies.	
We cut down the forest where these animals live so we can use the wood from the trees and build farms on the land.	
These animals have a horn like an elephant's tusk. We kill them to make medicine from the horn.	

WHO KILLS THESE ANIMALS? WE DO!

After Reading

Language

1 **Complete the sentences using the past simple or the present perfect of the verbs in brackets.**

a Dan .... (not visit) Hong Kong before.

b Dan .... (ask) Laura Chan some questions about ivory.

c Makenga .... (see) Dan and Sue following him.

d Makenga and Kimoti .... (be) to Hong Kong a number of times.

e Sue .... (not want) to follow Makenga and Kimoti.

f Sergeant Wong .... (know) about Makenga and Kimoti for some time.

2 **Words that go together. Match a word from Box A and a word from Box B. Then complete the sentences below.**

A

ivory
shop
apartment
newspaper
business
police

B

officer
block
window
trader
article
card

a Michael and Tanya Li live in an .... on the Peak.

b Laura Chan's .... says she is licensed to sell ivory.

c Laura Chan is an .... in Hong Kong.

d Sergeant Wong is a .... in the Hong Kong police.

e Dan and Sue watch Chan and Makenga through the ....

f Dan finds a .... about Makenga in South Africa.

3 Complete these sentences with the correct prepositions from the box.

> to   for   in   on   through   from

a Chinese people often eat dim sum .... breakfast.
b Dan and Sue heard about the killing of elephants .... the radio.
c Dan and Sue walked .... the streets, enjoying the sights and sounds.
d A tall African man was opening the door .... the ivory shop.
e Where do elephants come .... ?
f 'Look at that T-shirt,' she said .... her normal voice.

4 Use the words from the story to complete the sentences below.

> report   get away   sights   illegal   evidence   cross

a Dan was sure that Makenga was doing something ....
b Tanya Li told Sue to show Dan the .... of Hong Kong.
c Sue was .... because Dan didn't listen to her.
d Sergeant Wong thought Makenga was breaking the law but she had no ....
e Sue tried to .... from Kimoti but he was too strong.
f Sue wanted Dan to .... Makenga to the police, not to follow him.

73

After Reading

Exit Test

1 Listen and tick (✔) the correct picture.

K **2 Read the sentences and choose the best words 1, 2 or 3.**

a Tanya Li is ....
1 English **2** Chinese **3** half-English and half-Chinese

b When Dan and Sue first see Laura Chan's shop, they ....
1 go in and talk to her
2 watch her through the window
3 wait across the street

c Why does Dan want to watch Makenga? Because ....
1 he is carrying a bag
2 he looks unfriendly
3 he comes from Africa where there are elephants

d Kyle Pienaar tells Dan to ....
1 go to the police
2 keep away from Makenga
3 take some more photos of Makenga

e Makenga and Kimoti ....
1 go into Chungking Mansions
2 go into the Peninsula Hotel
3 get into a Rolls Royce

f Sergeant Wong ....
1 arrives too late to help Dan and Sue
2 takes Dan and Sue back to the Li's apartment
3 tells her officers to take Makenga and Kimoti away

3 Look at the pictures on pages 19 and 32. Ask and answer questions about what you can see and what the people are doing.

Who can you see?
What's he/she doing?

I can see...
He's/She's...

75

After Reading

Project **Animal Fact Files**

1 Read these facts about elephants.

TEN THINGS YOU DIDN'T KNOW ABOUT ELEPHANTS!

- There are two kinds of elephant: African and Asian.
- Elephants are the largest land animals in the world.
- The largest elephant ever weighed over 10,000 kg and was almost 4 metres high.
- An elephant's trunk can be 2 metres long.
- An elephant uses its trunk to put food and water into its mouth.
- It can use its tusks to dig in the ground for water.
- Its skin can be 2.5 cm thick.
- Elephants don't eat meat.
- They can swim.
- They can also cry, and play, and laugh, and they have very good memories.

WEB 2 Find out ten things about a different kind of animal: maybe a tiger, or a rhino or another animal you like. Use the Internet to help you.

Ten things you didn't know about…!